The Nightlight Knight

Belinda Karman
Seth Rowanwood

Belinda Karman (BA in Psy. & Art; MEd.), a parent of two, is a lifelong educator lovingly known as "Miss Belle" by some. While following her life path from Hong Kong, U.S.A., U.K., and Singapore to Canada, she holds fast her dedication to the continual healing and development at both the personal and collective levels. This commitment has led to her learning and adapting her works intuitively from healing modalities such as craniosacral therapy, restorative yoga, energy healing, hypnotherapy, personal training, to now publishing books for the children around us and within us. www.livingrestorative.com

Seth Rowanwood, a parent of one, is an award-winning artist, most notable for winning two Illustrator of the Future Contest Awards. The cover art he created for the book "Sliver Linings" went into space aboard the last Atlantis Space Shuttle flight 33! Seth's passion in life is to expand and share his understanding of verbal and non-verbal expression, such as in visual arts, design, music and literary arts. www.sethjrowanwood.com

Written by Belinda Karman
Illustrated by Seth Rowanwood
Edited by Kristen Allen

ISBN: 978-1-7778058-2-1

The Nightlight Knight

Belinda Karman

Seth Rowanwood

Other Books Published by Living Restorative

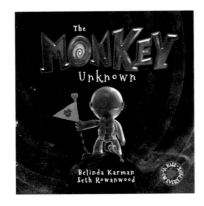

Hi!

My name is Bri!

I am a tyke-knight:

Not the shining-armour type,

But a Nightlight Knight!

I fight on my quike-kite

With my pike on my right,

And my nightlights tied tight

On my head and dyed tights.

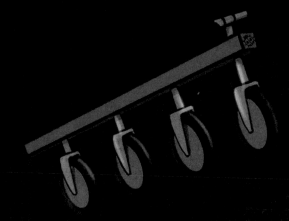

Never do I fight in daylight,

All my fights start after midnight.

What is it that I fight each night?

The limy slime that chimes like dimes!

It's alright to climb up The Thwype, yet
It's a high crime to be chiming like dimes.
So, fight, I must, this slime time after time,
To stop it from doing this nightly crime!

Why is it not fine to chime like some dimes?
No one in any tribe could utter why.
But here I am, the only one alive,
Assigned to fight this limy, dime-y slime.

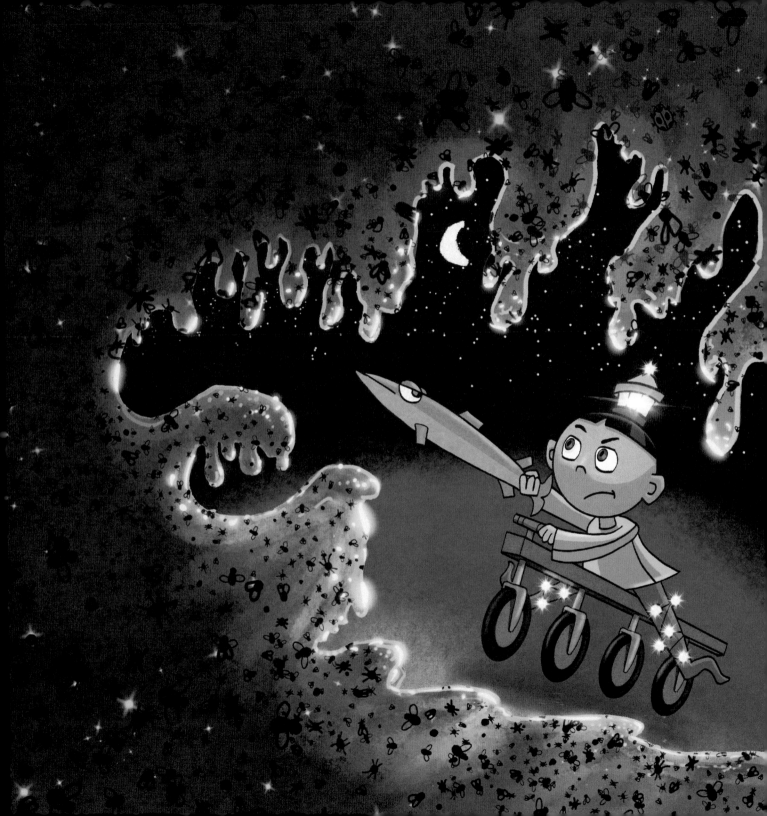

Every midnight with my pike and quike-kite,

I ride and hike with my trusty nightlights,

Fighting this feisty slime with all my might,

Just to stop it from chiming through the night.

But before the dark night turns into light,

I must take flight with my white striped quike-kite,

Nine miles away from this sly, chiming slime.

Right when sunlight turns it into a pie.

Away from this pie I must fly and hide,

Away from it I must divert my eyes.

'Cause whoever catches sight of this pie,

Would dine on it for five days and five nights

Except this sly pie is not made of slime,
Nor is it made of shiny dimes or limes.

It would fill your tummy with tiny lice,
A zillion mites, a jillion flies...

From then you can't ever dine or sigh,
You cannot ever recite your rhymes.

You shouldn't try to jive with a lyre,
You won't be able to sing a line.

You'd have to sign when you can't say, "Hi,"
And hide when it's time to say, "Bye-bye!"

For whenever your mouth's opened wide,
Tiny flies would fly right out in lines.

Never after should you ever cry,

Ne'er forever should you ever try.

You will forever have to mime,

Until the very day you die.

Last Friday, I lined up those tiny flies,
Brined them with mites, chives, thyme, and rind of limes.
Under the twilight I served them with fries,
Where the slime monster and I'd fight each night.

To my big delight the fight didn't start,
Nor the chimes of pennies, nickels, or dimes.
All night, we dined in kind on flies and fries,
Plus, the fireflies that light up the slime.

A pie it was not when the sunlight shined,

Still slime, I did find it, with a wild smile.

Things were fine since then with no more high crime,

My quarters are now a home for the slime.

Brining, drying, and frying the flies

Every day after reading some rhymes.

Each night, we dine and jive with the pike,

Then fly to new heights with fireflies.

To Big+ & 3(oo), thank you for showing me my monsters. -B

To Thi Thai, thank you for helping me accept my monsters. -B

To Maggs for all your support -S

Made in the USA
Columbia, SC
19 October 2021

47324353R00020